Dreamer

Inspired by a true story

By Tracey West

Based on the motion picture written by John Gatins

Scholastic Inc.

New York   Toronto   London   Auckland   Sydney
Mexico City   New Delhi   Hong Kong   Buenos Aires

ISBN: 0-439-77495-0

TM & © 2005 DreamWorks LLC

Published by Scholastic Inc.
SCHOLASTIC and associated logos are trademarks
and/or registered trademarks of Scholastic Inc.

12 11 10 9 8 7 6 5 4 3 2 1   5 6 7 8 9 10/0

Printed in the U.S.A.
First printing, October 2005

Cale Crane woke up early. The sun wasn't even up yet.

But Cale did not care. She wanted to go to work with her dad. She hoped he would finally let her.

Cale and her family lived on a horse farm. Cale loved horses! And her dad, Ben, was a horse trainer.

Today was a big day. Race day!
She'd get to see the horses run and
spend time with her dad. Cale watched
the horses warm up for the big race.

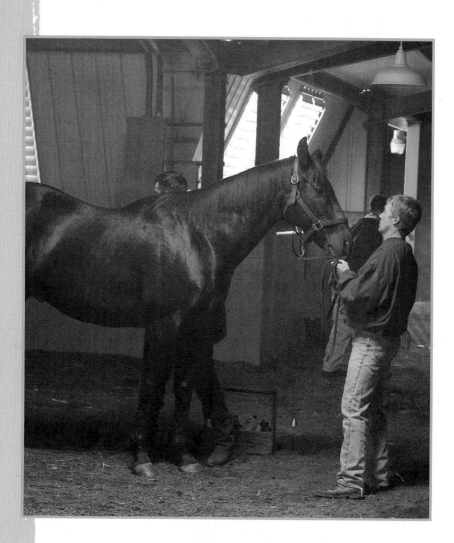

Ben took Cale to the stables. A stable worker walked a big horse named Goliath's Boy. Cale was scared of the black stallion.

A beautiful chestnut horse nuzzled
Cale's pocket.

"Sonya likes candy," said a groomer.

Cale took some candy from her pocket
and fed it to Sonya.

Ben walked Sonya back to her stall and felt her legs.

"Something is wrong," Ben said. "Sonya does not want to race."

"Of course she is going to race today," a voice said.

Ben's boss, Palmer, walked into the stable.

"Just do your job," Palmer said. "You work for me, remember?"

Ben had no choice. Cale watched the horses line up to race.

Would Sonya be okay?

Sonya tore around the racetrack. She ran faster and faster.

She raced toward the finish line . . . and then she fell!

Ben and the vet crew ran onto the track. It was bad news.

Sonya had broken her leg!

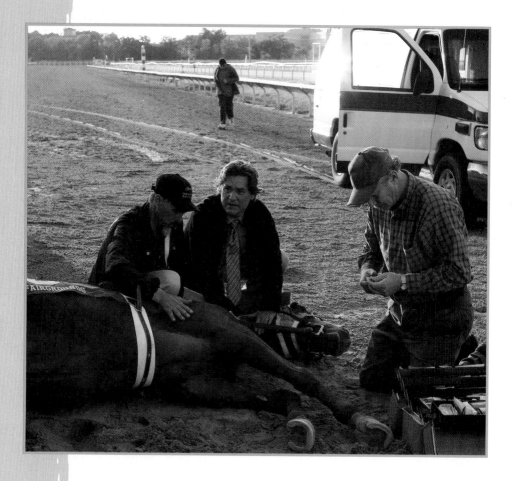

Palmer was angry with Ben.
"You are fired!" he yelled.
Ben was angry. Palmer owed him money.
So he made a deal.
"I want the horse," Ben said.

They brought Sonya back to the Cranes' farm. Ben stayed up all night taking care of her.

Cale was excited. She had always dreamed of having a horse of her own. Now the Cranes had a horse. But Sonya was badly hurt.

The next morning, Cale snuck out of her room. She wanted to see if Sonya was okay. Cale heard Doc Fleming talk to her dad. "Sonya will never race again," the vet said.

Cale knew that was bad news. What could Sonya do if she couldn't race?

Maybe they could make Sonya better. Ben put Sonya in a harness so her broken leg could heal.

That afternoon, Cale went to see Sonya.
Cale fell into the stall, and Sonya got scared.
"Leave her alone for now, Cale," Ben said.
"She is not a pet."

But Cale could not stay away. Every night, she went to the stables to see Sonya. She fed the horse sweet Popsicles through the slats of her stall.

Slowly, Sonya got better. Ben let Cale brush Sonya.

"That's it, Sonador," Ben said.

"Sonya door?" Cale asked.

"That's Sonya's full name. It's Spanish," Ben said. "It means 'Dreamer.'"

Cale finished brushing Sonya. "Good night, Dreamer," she said.

That night, a bad storm struck the farm. Sonya got scared. None of the men could get close to her.

But Cale calmed Sonya down. Ben watched, amazed. Cale and the horse had become good friends.

Finally, Sonya could walk on her own. Cale was happy. But then she heard her parents talking.

"I lost my job because of Sonya," Ben said. "Taking care of her costs money. I should not have done it. I only did it because Cale was with me."

Cale's eyes filled with tears. She ran to the barn.

"Okay, girl," she told Sonya. "We're going to run away. We're going to run far away."

Cale rode Sonya out of the barn. Ben saw them and yelled.

Sonya got scared. She began to run!

Sonya was running so fast that Cale could not hold on! Ben raced up in his truck. He pulled Cale off of Sonya and gave her a big hug. He was so happy that she was safe.

Ben and Cale were surprised by how fast Sonya had run.

Doc Fleming looked the horse over.

"Her leg is strong enough to race," the vet said. "But it's up to you."

"It's up to Cale," Ben said. "She is Sonya's new owner!"

Cale could not believe it. Sonya was all hers. And she was ready to race again —like she was born to do.

But first, Cale needed her father's help to train Sonya.

"I think Sonya should race in the Breeders' Cup Championships," Cale said.

The Breeders' Cup was a big race. Cale knew it was a big dream.

But Cale was a dreamer—just like Sonya.

Cale knew that it wouldn't be easy.
Only the best horses got to enter the race.
But she believed that Sonya could win.

Cale had to ask the Breeders' Cup chairman if Sonya could race.

He said Sonya could enter. But the fee to race was $120,000!

Cale was happy and sad at the same time. How could she ever get that much money?

Ben had an idea. He took Cale to see Prince Sadir.

"My horse will beat every horse in the race," Cale said. "Even Prince Tariq's horse."

Prince Sadir wanted his brother's horse, Goliath's Boy, to lose.

"I will give you the money," he said. "Pay me back—if you win."

The day of the big race came quickly. Cale helped get Sonya ready in the saddling area.

But then Palmer walked up with Goliath's Boy. The big horse lunged at Sonya. Sonya slammed into a fence. "Put her in the barn," Cale said sadly. She didn't want Sonya to get hurt. Not again.

But Sonya wouldn't go back.

"She wants to run," Ben said.

    While Sonya went to the starting gate,
Cale went to the owner's box with her
family. The race was about to begin!

The starting bell rang. Sonya raced out of the gate.

Goliath's Boy was in the lead. Sonya stayed right behind him.

But at the last minute, she flew past Goliath's Boy.

"Sonador wins!" the announcer yelled.

Ben put Cale on Sonya's back. He led the pair around the winner's circle. Sonya was covered in ribbons and flowers. In one split second, all of Cale's dreams had come true. Thanks to a horse named Dreamer!